My Weird School Special

Bunny Double, We're in Trouble!

Dan Gutman

Pictures by
Jim Paillot

HARPER

An Imprint of HarperCollinsPublishers

To Emma

My Weird School Special: Bunny Double, We're in Trouble!
Text copyright © 2014 by Dan Gutman
Illustrations copyright © 2014 by Jim Paillot

Library of Congress catalog card number: 2013032165
ISBN 978-0-06-228401-3 (lib. bdg.) — ISBN 978-0-06-228400-6 (pbk. bdg.)

Typography by Kate Engbring
19   CG/LSCH   10 9 8 7 6 5 4 3
❖
First Edition

Contents

How to Look Like a Dork

My name is A.J. and I hate wearing a tie.

Ties are *horrible*! Who came up with the idea that boys should wear a skinny piece of cloth around their neck on holidays? That was the dumbest idea in the history of the world.

"Wake up, A.J.!" my mom shouted from

downstairs. "Get dressed! Don't forget to put on your new shirt and tie."

What?

I opened my eyes. It was *Sunday*. There was no school. We were on spring vacation. Why did I need to get dressed up?

"Do I have to?" I yelled.

"It's *Easter*, A.J.," my dad shouted. "Show your respect."

Respect? Why is it respectful to wear a string around your neck? That makes no sense at all. When I grow up, I'm going to be a professional skateboarder. Skateboarders don't wear ties. They wear sneakers and ripped jeans.

I got up and put on my new shirt. Then I put on my dumb tie.

Well, I *tried* to put on my dumb tie. My dad once showed me how to tie a tie, but I didn't remember very well. I put the fat end over the skinny end and looped it around. No, that wasn't right. Then I tried putting the skinny end over the fat end and looped it around. That wasn't right either.

How do you tie a tie anyway? Ties are impossible to tie.

"Hurry up, A.J.!" my mom yelled from downstairs. "We have to *go!*"

I tried to tie the tie every which way. Nothing worked. It looked like a bird's nest hanging around my neck. This was going to be the worst day of my life.

That's when Dad came into my room to

see what was taking me so long. He was wearing his nice suit.

"This tie is broken," I told him. "It doesn't work right."

"Here, buddy," Dad said. "Let me help you with that."

My dad stood behind me and tied the tie in like two seconds. He pulled the knot all the way up to the top.

"Gak! You're choking me!" I gagged. "The tie . . . is cutting off the air supply . . .

to my brain. Need . . . oxygen. Feel . . . woozy. Everything . . . spinning. I think I'm gonna . . . pass out! Must go back . . . to bed."

"Oh, stop being so dramatic," Dad said. "Let's go downstairs."

When we got to the top of the stairs, my mom looked up at me. A big smile spread across her face.

"You look very handsome and grown up, A.J.!"

"I look like a dork," I said.*

---

*So how are you enjoying the story so far? Can we get you a pillow or something to make this reading experience more pleasurable?

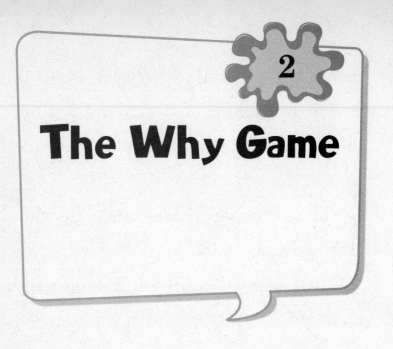

The Why Game

My older sister, Amy, was already downstairs. She was all dolled up in her pink dress, white shoes, and a frilly Easter bonnet. My mom was dressed up fancy too. It looked like we were all going to a funeral.

"Okay, let's go!" my dad said.

"Do I *have* to go?" I asked.

"Yes, you have to go, A.J.," said my mom.

"Why?" I asked.

"Because it's Easter, and this is what we do on Easter," said my dad.

"Why?" I asked again.

If you don't want to do something, try playing The Why Game. It's fun! Here's how you play: no matter what your mom or dad says, just keep asking "Why?" It drives grown-ups crazy. Sometimes The Why Game can go on for hours.

"We have to go because it's a family tradition," said my mom.

"Why?" I asked.

"It just *is*," said my dad.

"Why?"

"Because I said so," my dad barked.

"That's not fair," I whined.

The Why Game always ends with the grown-up barking "Because I said so," and then you have to whine, "That's not fair." Nobody knows why.

"I'll take care of this," Amy announced. She pulled me to the side.

"It's Easter, dumbhead!" Amy whispered in my ear. "Don't you know what that means?"

"It means I have to wear a tie?"

"No!" Amy whispered. "It means you get to eat lots of *candy*."

Oh, *yeaaaaahhhhh*! I forgot about that. *Now* she was talking my language.

"They're going to have tons of chocolate," Amy whispered. "And marshmallows! And Peeps!"

PEEPS?

Did she say Peeps? My name is A.J. and I *love* Peeps!

In case you live in a cave where they don't sell Peeps, they are these delicious marshmallow candies shaped like chicks and bunnies. They're coated with sugar, which is my favorite food.

You can put sugar on just about *anything* to make it taste good. I bet that if you covered a clump of dirt with sugar, it would probably taste good. Not that I'm going to eat dirt or anything. But I bet my friend Ryan would eat a sugar-coated dirt clump. He'll eat *anything,* even stuff that isn't food.

Marshmallows are already made of

sugar, so they taste great. But then they put even *more* sugar on them to turn them into Peeps, and that makes them taste even *better* than a plain marshmallow. I bet that if you took a Peep and sprinkled even *more* sugar on it, it would taste even *better* than a plain Peep. I should try that sometime.

The point is that Peeps are the greatest invention in the history of the world.* The person who invented Peeps should get the Nobel Prize. That's a prize they give out to people who don't have bells. And the best part is that on Easter you can eat all the Peeps you want—no questions asked.

I have learned a lot about life in my eight years. Sometimes you have to take the bad with the good. If you want to get really great at skateboarding, you have to spend *hours and hours* practicing. If you

*Well, I guess the lightbulb was pretty good, too. But it would be weird to eat lightbulbs.

want to get great grades in school, you have to spend *hours and hours* studying. And if you want to eat Peeps, you have to wear a dumb string around your neck for *hours and hours*.

"Let's go!" I said, charging out the door.

This was going to be the best day of my life!

Me and My Peeps

After we drove a million hundred miles, my dad pulled the car into the driveway of a gigantic mansion. It looked like the White House.

"WOW," I said, which is "MOM" upside down. "Who lives in this place, the president of the United States?"

"No, this is Mayor Hubble's house," my mom told me.

Mayor Hubble! He used to be the mayor of our town. But then he got in trouble by stealing money. I heard he was in jail.

"The mayor cares so deeply about our town," Mom told me, "that he wanted to have an Easter celebration at his house even though he can't be here himself."

We walked inside. The place looked like a museum. There were paintings of Mayor Hubble hanging on the walls, and lots of servants too.

Well, the servants weren't hanging on the walls. That would be weird.

There were so many servants that I think some of the servants had servants.

And they were all wearing tuxedos. Hey, how come guys in tuxedos look like penguins? What's up with that?

The place was *really* fancy. I was afraid to touch anything or sit in a chair because a SWAT team might come running in and arrest me. Some musicians wearing tuxedos were playing that song "A-Tisket, A-Tasket," which makes no sense at all. What's a tasket? I bet they just made up that word because they couldn't think of anything else that rhymed with "basket."

"Welcome to Hubble Manor," one of those servant guys said to us. "If I can do anything to make your visit here more enjoyable, please do not hesitate to ask."

"Where are the Peeps?" I asked.

"That's *rude*, A.J.!" my mom told me. "You don't ask where the Peeps are! They'll give out Peeps when they're good and ready to give out Peeps."

Mom was really mad. We walked around for a few minutes until some other servant guy came over. He was carrying a plate of food.

"Or derves?" he asked.

I didn't know what "or derves" were, but they looked yucky.

"Man, you could get *lost* in this place," my dad said as he picked up one of those or derve things.

"Hubble Manor has thirty-four bedrooms," said the or derve guy, "a library, a helicopter pad, twenty-three bathrooms . . ."

Twenty-three bathrooms?! Was he joking? My house only has two bathrooms. Mayor Hubble must have to go to the bathroom *all* the time. He should see a doctor about that instead of putting bathrooms all over his house.

". . . and four half bathrooms," said the or derve guy.

"Half bathrooms?" I asked. "Why would anybody want *half* of a bathroom? What could you do with half a toilet bowl?"

"A half bathroom is a powder room, sir," the guy told me.

Powder room?

"Mayor Hubble needs a whole *room* to hold powder?" I asked. "Why can't he just keep powder in a little box like normal people?"

"Hmmm, most amusing," said the or derve guy as he walked away. "If you folks need anything, I am at your disposal."

Disposal? What was he talking about? I didn't bring a garbage can with me.

That guy was weird.

We walked down a gigantic hallway that was filled with statues of Mayor Hubble. The hallway led to the backyard, where a lot of people were hanging around. The whole gang was there. I spotted my friends

Michael, Ryan, Alexia, and Neil. Everybody was all dressed up, even Alexia. She's a tomboy, and she *never* wears a dress.

That's when I saw the most horrible thing in the history of the world.

Andrea Young!

She is this annoying girl in my class with curly brown hair. Andrea was giggling with her crybaby friend Emily. They came running over.

"Hi Arlo!" Andrea said. She calls me by my real name because she knows I don't like it. "What do you think of my new dress?"

Andrea spun around to show off her dumb dress. Ugh, disgusting!

I was about to say something mean, but my mother gave me a look and said, "It's *lovely*, Andrea!"

"I do just *love* getting dressed up in fancy clothes!" Andrea gushed. "Did you see my corsage?"

"I *love* it!" said Emily, who always agrees with everything Andrea says. "Did you see mine?"

"I *love* it!" said Andrea.

Andrea and Emily were saying the *L* word way too much. I thought I was gonna throw up.

My parents went to some fancy room to drink coffee and talk about the weather with the other grown-ups. That's what they do when there are no kids around. Nobody knows why.

Me and the guys and Alexia went out on the back lawn. It was *huge*.

"Man, you could play football out here," I said.

"I *wish* we could play football here," said Michael, "instead of doing *this* stuff."

One of those servant guys must have heard us, because he came over.

"Actually," he told us, "this lawn used to *be* a football field years ago. If you look carefully, you can still see the lines on the grass."

He was right. It would be *cool* to play football on Mayor Hubble's lawn. But that would have been impossible because it was filled with kids flying kites, playing with Hula-Hoops, and getting their faces painted. There were jugglers, clowns, guys playing banjos, storytellers, and all kinds of activities.

"Mayor Hubble sure knows how to throw a party," said Ryan.

"Did you guys see any Peeps?" asked Alexia.

"Yeah," I said. "Where are the Peeps? Peeps are *awesome*."

"I could eat heaps of Peeps," said Michael, who never ties his shoes.

"I could eat Peeps in my sleep," said Neil, who we call the nude kid even though he wears clothes.

"Only creeps don't like Peeps," said Alexia.

"I weep if I don't get Peeps," said Ryan.

"I wish I was knee deep in—"

I didn't get the chance to finish my sentence, because at that moment the most amazing thing in the history of the world happened. We heard a noise up in the sky.

Well, that wasn't the amazing part. We

hear noises up in the sky all the time. The amazing part was that the noise was a helicopter, and it was coming down on the lawn!

Everybody pointed up in the air. The helicopter landed on a big circle at the far end of the grass. The propellers stopped spinning, and the door opened.

"I think it's the president!" some kid yelled.

"No, it's the pope!" yelled some other kid.

"No, it's Chuck Norris!" a third kid yelled.

They were all wrong. The guy who came out of the helicopter was . . . Mayor Hubble!

Mayor Hubble Is No Longer in Trouble

We all ran over to the helicopter. This was *exciting*! Mayor Hubble is an important man. He's like the king of the world. It wasn't every day that we got to see such a famous person.

A big cheer went up as Mayor Hubble stepped off the helicopter and waved to the crowd. His bodyguards came running over. They were big guys in black shirts and sunglasses who looked mean. Some other guys came out in a line and started playing trumpets to welcome Mayor Hubble. A few servants rolled out a red carpet so Mayor Hubble wouldn't have to walk on the grass. A couple of other guys set up a podium for Mayor Hubble to stand behind.

Important people like Mayor Hubble always stand behind a podium when they talk. Nobody knows why. Mayor Hubble probably has a podium in his living room. It would be cool if he stood behind the podium in his living room and said something like . . .

"I have an important announcement to make. It is time for me to take out the garbage."

The principal of our school, Mr. Klutz, came running up to the podium. He has no hair at all. I mean *none*.

"Mayor Hubble!" said Mr. Klutz. "To what do we owe the pleasure of your company?* I thought you were in jail."

---

*That's grown-up talk for "What are you doing here?"

"I got time off for good behavior," replied Mayor Hubble. "I would *never* miss the annual Easter egg hunt."

All the kids gathered around the podium. Even the grown-ups came out of the house to listen to the mayor speak.

Suddenly, everybody got quiet.

"Welcome to Hubble Manor!" the mayor said into the microphone. "Today, my house is your house. This is the *people's* house!"

"Hooray for Mayor Hubble!" somebody shouted, and we all had to do that hip-hip-hooray thing.

Mayor Hubble took a sheet of paper out of his jacket and started to read his speech. . . .

"Friends, families, students, teachers, and parents," he said, "what a wonderful day this is! Spring is in the air. Every year at this time blah blah blah blah Easter blah blah blah blah renewal of life blah

blah blah blah blah blah blah blah flowers pushing up through the frosty ground
blah blah blah blah . . ."

What a snoozefest! He went on like that
for about a million hundred hours. I had
no idea what he was talking about. My
shirt was itchy. My tie was choking me. I
thought I was gonna die. All I could think
about was when Mayor Hubble would stop
talking so we could go eat some Peeps.

The Little Monsters

Everybody cheered when Mayor Hubble finished his speech. I wasn't sure if they were cheering because it was such a good speech or because it was *over*. Some guys rolled the red carpet back up and took away the podium.

"And now," said Mayor Hubble, "I would

like to introduce our hostess for the day, my lovely wife, Bubbles!"

Bubbles Hubble?

Mrs. Bubbles came running over. She looked like one of those ladies in a shampoo commercial who swirls her hair around in slow motion. Mrs. Bubbles had on a red dress and high heels. She gave the mayor a big kiss and told him how happy she was to see him again.

Ugh, disgusting!

"Hey, everybody!" Mrs. Bubbles announced. "Thanks for coming today! Are you ready for our annual egg roll?"

"Egg roll?" I shouted. "Yipee! I *love* Chinese food!"

"Not *that* kind of an egg roll, dumb-head," Andrea said to me, rolling her eyes. "In an egg roll, you roll eggs."

"I knew that," I lied.

Apparently, an egg roll is when a bunch of kids roll eggs along the grass. The first one to push the egg across a finish line is the winner. If you ask me, that had to be the dumb-est contest in the history of the world. What's the point of rolling an egg around somebody's lawn?

"I'm not doing that," said Michael. "That's for *little* kids."

"Me neither," said Ryan and Neil.

Andrea and Emily said they didn't want to get dirt on their new dresses.

"The winner of the egg roll will receive a prize," announced Mrs. Bubbles. "The first child to push his or her egg across the finish line will receive a wooden egg, personally autographed by Mayor Hubble and me."

Mrs. Bubbles held up the wooden egg.

"Wooden egg?" Alexia whispered to me. "Where do you think she got a wooden egg?"

"From a wooden chicken," I guessed.

Alexia and I decided that it would be cool to win a wooden egg. We went over to the starting line. So did about a million first graders.

"Look at these little munchkins," I whispered to Alexia. "No way they're gonna beat us."

"This is gonna be a piece of cake," said Alexia.

I didn't know what cake had to do with anything. Why is everybody always talking about cake?

Mrs. Bubbles gave each of us a plastic egg and a long spoon. Then we went over to the starting line.

"Okay, is everybody ready?" said Mrs.

Bubbles. "On your mark . . . get set . . . let's ROLL!"

I thought that Alexia and I could just push those first-grade munchkins out of our way, but it was the other way around! They were like animals, yelling and screaming and pushing and shoving and crying and swinging their spoons every which way. It was like a war zone!

"Get out of my way!" some kid shouted.

"Watch out!"

"Mommy!"

"Oww! You hit me in the face with your spoon!"

I thought I was going to get trampled by those little monsters. They were brutal!

And they were actually *winning*!

If Alexia and I lost the egg roll, the gang would never stop making fun of us. That's when I came up with the greatest idea in the history of the world.

"Pssst!" I whispered to Alexia. "Let's just pick our eggs up and *throw* them across the finish line. Nobody will know."

"You should get the Nobel Prize for that idea," Alexia whispered back.

I bent down to pick up my egg. But before I could get it, one of those first-grade munchkin girls stomped on it.

CRACK.

My egg was all over the grass in a bunch of pieces.

"Hey, kid!" I shouted. "You busted my egg!"

But that munchkin didn't care. She was long gone. Some other little boy monster stepped on Alexia's egg and smashed it. He ended up winning the wooden egg.

After the egg roll was over, Michael and Ryan made fun of us for letting a bunch of first graders beat us.

I thought Mrs. Bubbles might give us some Peeps for participating in the egg roll. But she didn't.

"Maybe there's a Peep shortage," Alexia told me.

"Yeah, maybe they have to conserve the Peeps," Ryan said, "so there will still be Peeps left in a hundred years for our children and future generations to eat."

"The Peeps would be stale by then," said Neil.

"Stale Peeps are better than no Peeps," said Michael.

"Can't they just make *more* Peeps?" I asked.

"Okay, kids!" said Mrs. Bubbles. "Let's all go inside the house."

All right! Finally! It was Peeps time.

I Thought I Was Gonna Dye

Mrs. Bubbles led us inside Hubble Manor. There were separate rooms for the first graders, second graders, third graders, and fourth graders. Me and the gang went into the third-grade room. A long table was in there. And you'll never believe in a million hundred years who walked into the door at that moment.

Nobody! It would hurt if you walked into a door. But you'll never believe who walked into the door*way*.

It was our art teacher from school, Ms. Hannah! She never throws anything away, because she says *everything* can be art. Ms. Hannah was wearing an Easter dress made out of old pot holders.

"What are *you* doing here, Ms. Hannah?" asked Neil.

"Are you going to pass out the Peeps?" asked Alexia.

"We want Peeps!" I shouted, jumping up from my seat. "We want Peeps!"

I figured *everybody* would jump up from

their seats and start chanting "We want Peeps!" with me.

I looked around. Nobody else was standing. Nobody else was chanting. Everybody was looking at me.

Well, *that* was embarrassing. I sat back down in my seat.

"No, I'm not here to pass out Peeps," said Ms. Hannah. "I'm going to help you do Easter egg dyeing!"

What?!

"I thought Easter eggs were *already* dead," I said.

Everybody laughed even though I didn't say anything funny.

"Not *that* kind of dying, dumbhead!" Andrea said, rolling her eyes. "We're going to dye eggs in different colors. It's my favorite thing to do in the whole *world*!"

"Mine too!" shouted Emily. She jumped up in the air and started hugging Andrea.

Everything those two do is their favorite thing to do in the whole world. What is their problem? Why can't a truck full of Easter eggs fall on their heads?

We all sat down at the long table. Ms. Hannah got out a bunch of eggs and cups and other stuff from a cabinet. She put a colored tablet into each cup and then poured water and vinegar into the cups.

Ugh! The vinegar smelled *horrible*! I thought I was gonna dye. I mean die.

We put our eggs on these little wire things so we could dip them into the cups. Ms. Hannah showed us how we could put stickers on the eggs or wrap rubber bands around them so the dye would only color certain parts of the egg.

It was pretty cool, I had to admit. We dyed a lot of eggs. At the end, our fingers were all different colors.

We had to wait a few minutes for our eggs to dry, so Ms. Hannah had us sing this song called "Little Bunny Foo Foo." Did you ever hear that song? It's about this rabbit that goes hopping through the forest. It sees a bunch of field mice that were minding their own business, and it starts bopping them on the head for no reason!*

That song is weird. We had to sing it about five million times.

Then Ms. Hannah got out crayons so we could draw pictures on our dyed eggs.

"I'm going to draw a pretty butterfly," said Andrea.

"Me too!" said Emily.

"I'm going to draw an elephant stomping on two butterflies," I said.

"You're mean, Arlo!" Andrea said.

Ms. Hannah started singing that Bunny

*He probably went crazy because his parents named him Foo Foo. What kind of a name is Foo Foo? I'll bet all the other rabbits made fun of him at school. If my parents named me Foo Foo, I would run away to Antarctica to go live with the penguins.

Foo Foo song again. And you'll never believe who poked his head into the door at that moment.

Nobody! It would hurt if you poked your head into a door. I thought we went over that already.

But you'll never believe who poked his head into the door*way*.

I'm not going to tell you.

Okay, okay, I'll tell you. But you have to read the next chapter. So nah-nah-nah boo-boo on you.

The Easter Bunny Is Weird

It was Mr. Klutz who poked his head into the doorway!

"Are you all having a good time?" he asked.

"Yes!" shouted all the girls except for Alexia.

"No!" shouted all the boys and Alexia.

"This looks like fun," said Mr. Klutz.

"Did you ever dye Easter eggs, Mr. Klutz?" asked Ryan.

"Sure I did," he replied. "I was a boy once, you know."

"Only once?" I asked. "I'm a boy *all* the time."

Everybody laughed even though I didn't say anything funny.

Mr. Klutz leaned down so he could get a good look at our colored eggs. That's when I noticed something. Mr. Klutz's head looked just like an *egg*!

"Hey Mr. Klutz," I said, "can we dye your head?"

Well, it was like I said a bad word or

something. All the kids stopped talking. Mr. Klutz looked at me. Ms. Hannah looked at me. *Everybody* was looking at me. I thought I heard crickets chirping.

"I'll make a deal with you, A.J.," Mr. Klutz told me. "I'll let you dye my head . . . *if* you can recite the eight times table."

Hmmm. We were learning the eight times table at school. I wasn't sure if I remembered the whole thing.

"Eight times one is eight," I said. "Because one eight can only be eight. Any dumbhead knows that."

"Right," said Mr. Klutz.

"Eight times two is sixteen," I said. "Because eight plus eight is sixteen."

"Yes . . ."

"Eight times three is . . . twenty-four," I said, adding another eight.

"Um-hmm."

"Eight times four is . . ."

"Thirty-two," Andrea whispered in my ear.

"Thirty-two," I said.

I kept going. Some of them I knew, and some of them I didn't.

When I didn't know an answer, Andrea or Emily whispered it in my ear. Finally, I got to the end.

". . . and eight times ten is . . . eighty!" I said.

"That's right!" said Mr. Klutz. "Now you may dye my head."

We couldn't dip Mr. Klutz's head into a cup because it was too big. Ms. Hannah gave us Q-tips so we could dab the dye on Mr. Klutz. We had a great time dyeing his head red, white, blue, and green. When the dye was dry, Andrea drew a butterfly right in the middle. It looked cool.

After that Mr. Klutz left, and he took his dyed head with him.

It was cleanup time. While we cleaned up, Ms. Hannah turned on a boom box, and the song "Here Comes Peter Cottontail" started playing.

"Hey, guess who's coming, kids?" asked Ms. Hannah.

"Santa Claus?" I asked.

"Santa comes at Christmas, dumbhead!" said Andrea.

"Oh, snap!" said Ryan.

I was going to say "So is your face" to Andrea, but you'll never believe in a million hundred years who walked into the door at that moment.

It was a giant Easter Bunny! He walked right into the door!

"Ouch!" the Easter Bunny yelled. "Who put this door here? I can't see through this stupid bunny head."

That voice sounded familiar. I knew I had heard it before.

"Hey, the Easter Bunny isn't supposed to talk!" said Michael.

"Oh, yeah, I forgot," said the Easter Bunny.

"And he's not supposed to say the word 'stupid,'" said Andrea. "That's not a nice word."

"Sorry!"

A bunch of grown-ups crowded around the door and started taking pictures. Like they never saw a guy dressed up as a bunny before, right?

The Easter Bunny was carrying a basket. I got up on my tiptoes to see if there were any Peeps in the basket, but the only thing in it was a bunch of fake green plastic grass. What's up with *that* stuff?

"Do you have any Peeps?" I asked.

"Sorry, kid," said the Easter Bunny. "I'm not allowed to talk."

And then he hopped away.

"I thought the Easter Bunny was supposed to give us candy," said Neil the nude kid.

"If I don't get some candy soon, I'm gonna pass out," said Michael.

They were right. It was Easter, and so far we didn't get *any* candy. No chocolate. No marshmallows. No Peeps. No *nothing*. All we did was roll eggs around the grass and dye them.

"Y'know," I said to the gang, "something tells me that guy was not the *real* Easter Bunny."

"What do you mean?" asked Ryan.

"He's probably a lunatic who kidnapped the real Easter Bunny, stole his costume, and tied him to the railroad tracks on the outskirts of town," I said. "That stuff happens all the time, you know."

"Arlo, stop trying to scare Emily," said Andrea.

"I'm scared," said Emily.

I thought Emily was going to start crying and run out of the room like she usually does. But as it turned out, we *all* went running out of the room.

"Everybody come outside!" Mrs. Bubbles shouted. "It's time for the big Easter egg hunt!"

The Golden Egg

While we were inside that whole time, the grown-ups must have been outside hiding Easter eggs. Everybody ran out of the room and gathered on the back porch around Mayor Hubble and Mrs. Bubbles.

"Okay, kids," said the mayor, "there are

hundreds of plastic eggs scattered all over the lawn."

"And there's a little something *special* for you inside each one of them," said Mrs. Bubbles.

Me and the gang all looked at each other and mouthed the word "candy." I licked my lips. *Finally*, we were going to get candy. It was about time! The servant guys came around, handing out empty bags to everyone.

"Oh, one thing we should mention," Mrs. Bubbles said. "There's one *special* egg. It's a *golden* egg."

"Oooooh!" everybody said, because golden stuff is always cool.

"What's special about the golden egg?" Ryan shouted.

"You know the Burger Queen next to the mall?" asked Mayor Hubble. "I talked them into sponsoring this year's golden Easter egg."

"Sponsor? What does that mean?" asked Michael.

"It means that if you open up the golden egg," said Mrs. Bubbles, "you'll find some hundred-dollar bills inside. They were donated by Burger Queen."

"WOW," everybody said, which is "MOM" upside down.

"How *many* hundred-dollar bills?" one of the grown-ups shouted.

"Ten," said Mayor Hubble.

Ten hundred-dollar bills? I'm glad we studied the ten times table in school. Ten times a hundred is . . . uh . . . Add a zero. . . . Um . . . No, add two zeroes. . . . No, that's not it. . . .

"A thousand dollars!" Andrea shouted.

A thousand dollars? That's almost a million!

"WOW," everybody said, which is "MOM" upside down.

"Yes!" said Mrs. Bubbles. "One of you is going to go home today with a thousand dollars!"

Everybody was excited, even the grown-ups. Suddenly, they all stopped drinking coffee and talking about the weather. They were putting their cups down and inching closer to the lawn. There was electricity in the air!*

"On your mark," said the mayor, ". . . get set . . . GO GET 'EM! GO GET THOSE EGGS!"

Mrs. Bubbles blew a whistle, and the next thing I knew, there were a million hundred people running all over the lawn.

"Out of my way!" somebody shouted.

"Let's go!"

"A thousand dollars!"

"Grab the eggs!"

---

*Well, not really. If there was electricity in the air, we all would have been electrocuted.

"Hurry up!"

Everybody was freaking out! It was like they were giving away free candy.

Oh, wait a minute. They *were* giving away free candy.

I ran out onto the lawn and spotted a few eggs that were behind a tree. I didn't even take the time to open them up to get the treats out before I scooped them up and put them in my bag. I wanted to find more eggs.

Those first graders were monsters at the egg roll, but you should have seen the *parents* at the egg hunt. They were all shoving each other, elbowing each other out of the way, tripping over each

other, and trampling over the flowers and bushes. They all had crazy looks in their eyes. I hadn't seen grown-ups act like this since the last time my dad was late for work and he couldn't find his car keys.

"I gotta find that golden egg!" some guy said as he shoved an old lady out of his way.

"Not if I find it first!" said the old lady, who whacked the guy with her cane.

You should have *been* there! Those grown-ups were hilarious. If you ask me, grown-ups like money as much as kids like candy.

9

Don't Open That Door!

Everybody was running around the lawn like crazy people for about ten minutes. I got five eggs myself. It looked like we had scooped up all of them, but so far nobody had found the *golden* egg. Grown-ups were still wandering around the lawn like zombies looking for it.

I went over to the porch, where the gang was standing. Andrea and Emily came over too.

"Let's open up our eggs and eat the candy," said Ryan.

"But the golden egg is still out there," said Michael. "If we eat our candy now, somebody else will find it."

"Where could it be?" asked Neil.

"We need to think outside the box," said Alexia.

I looked around. I didn't see any boxes.

"What do boxes have to do with anything?" I asked. "I wasn't even *inside* a box. How can you think inside a box anyway? It would have to be a really big box.

And there aren't any boxes around here—"

"Arlo, chill!" Andrea said. "There are hundreds of people out here on the lawn, right?"

"Right," we all said.

"And none of them can find the golden egg, right?"

"Right," we all said.

"So the golden egg must be hidden . . ."

"Inside the house!" Andrea and I said at the same time.

We all tiptoed inside Hubble Manor. None of the grown-ups noticed us, because they were all looking for the golden egg on the lawn.

There must be a million hundred doors

inside Hubble Manor. We started sneaking down a hallway like secret agents, hiding behind the curtains and giggling. It was cool.

"I bet there are some Peeps in here somewhere," Alexia said.

"If you were a Peep, where would you be?" asked Neil.

"In somebody's mouth," I said.

"Forget about the Peeps!" said Michael. "After we find the golden egg with a thousand dollars inside it, we can buy all the Peeps we want."

Good point.

"Shhhh!" said Andrea. "Somebody will hear us."

"I'm scared," said Emily. "We're going to get into trouble."

"Chillax," I told her. "Nobody said we couldn't look inside the house."

We walked up and down the hallways. When we passed by one door, I heard a noise. I stopped. The sound was coming from behind the door. I put my hand on the doorknob.

"Don't open that door, A.J.!" warned Ryan.

"Why not?" I asked.

"Whenever they open a door in a scary movie," Ryan said, "there's always a crazy guy hiding behind it with an ax."

"That's *ridiculous*," said Michael. "Believe me, there's no crazy guy hiding behind the door with an ax."

"You're right," I said. "He might have a chain saw."

"Stop trying to scare Emily," said Andrea.

"I'm scared," said Emily.

My hand was still on the doorknob. What if there really *was* a crazy guy with an ax or a chain saw hiding behind the

door? I was faced with the hardest decision of my life. I didn't know what to do. I looked at Alexia. Alexia looked at Ryan. Ryan looked at Michael. Michael looked at Neil. Neil looked at Andrea. Andrea looked at Emily. Everybody was looking at each other.

I took a deep breath.

I turned the doorknob.

I pushed open the door.

And you'll never believe in a million hundred years who was sitting in that room.

It was the Easter Bunny!

And he had no head!

The Last Peep

"Ahhhhhhhhhh!" we all screamed.

Not only did the Easter Bunny have his bunny head on the floor next to him, but the guy inside the Easter Bunny suit was somebody we all knew!

"You're not the Easter Bunny!" Michael

shouted. "You're Boomer Wiggins!"

Michael was right! Boomer Wiggins is a famous football player. He came to visit our class last year when our teacher was Miss Daisy. He is cool!

"Yeah, so what?" grunted Boomer Wiggins, letting out a burp.

"What are *you* doing dressed up like the Easter Bunny?" I asked.

"I retired from football last year," Boomer told us. "But I couldn't find a job anywhere. Nobody wanted to hire me. I applied to be Santa Claus, but they said I wasn't fat enough. I applied to be the tooth fairy, but they said I wasn't skinny enough. So I took this job."

Boomer looked sad. He had a big chocolate bunny in his bunny hand. He bit one
of the ears off. There were lots of candy
boxes scattered on the floor around the
chair Boomer Wiggins was sitting in.

So *that's* why we didn't get any candy! Boomer had it all.

"You'll get another job, Boomer," Andrea told him. "My mom always says that if you put your mind to it, you can do *anything*."

Boomer didn't look convinced.

"When I played football, kids used to ask me for autographs," he muttered as he bit off the bunny's other ear. "They used to send me fan letters. Not anymore. Nobody loves me."

"*We* love you, Boomer!" said Andrea.

"Yeah, we love you," said Emily.

I wasn't about to use the *L* word, but I went over and gave Boomer a hug. So did Alexia.

We told Boomer that he shouldn't be

ashamed to dress up as the Easter Bunny, because the Easter Bunny brings lots of joy to girls and boys. But that didn't seem to cheer him up any.

"Leave me alone," Boomer said. "Just let me sit here and stuff my face with junk food."

That's when the most amazing thing in the history of the world happened. Boomer reached into the pocket of his bunny costume, and you know what he pulled out?

A Peep!

"So *that's* where all the Peeps went!" I shouted.

"Boomer, you ate all the Peeps?" asked Alexia.

"I did not," Boomer replied. "I still have one left."

With that, he popped the Peep into his mouth.

"Noooooooooooooo!" we all shouted.

Boomer Wiggins ate the last Peep.

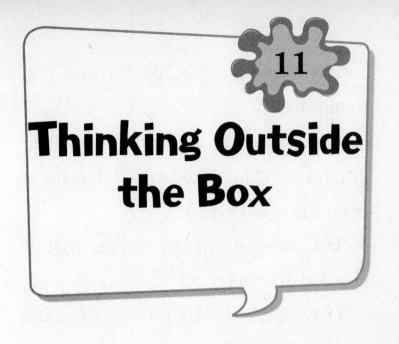

Thinking Outside the Box

We decided to leave Boomer alone and go back to the party so we could open our plastic eggs and eat the candy inside. But when we got to the lawn, the other kids were gathered around Mr. Klutz and Mrs. Bubbles. She was holding a big basket, and it was filled with all our eggs.

"Hey, those are *our* eggs!" I said. "We found them!"

"We're going to try something different this year," Mr. Klutz said. "I'm going to open the eggs for you."

"But we get what's inside, right?" shouted Michael.

"Of course," said Mrs. Bubbles. "You kids get the prizes."

Mr. Klutz opened an egg. I thought a piece of candy was going to fall out. But it didn't. You know what fell out?

A piece of paper!

WHAT?!

No candy?

"Each piece of paper has a question

written on it," said Mr. Klutz. "The first child to answer the question correctly will get a chocolate-covered marshmallow bunny!"

A chocolate-covered marshmallow bunny? Count me in. I *love* chocolate-covered marshmallow bunnies!

I looked at Andrea. Andrea looked at me. We both made mean faces at each other. There was no way Little Miss Know-It-All was going to win the chocolate-covered marshmallow bunnies.

"Okay," said Mr. Klutz as he opened the first egg. "What is . . . seven times eight?"

"Ninety-nine!" I yelled. "Ha! In your face, Andrea!"

"Fifty-six!" yelled Andrea.

"Right!" said Mr. Klutz. "Andrea gets a chocolate-covered marshmallow bunny."

"Oh, man!" I shouted.

No fair! Andrea went up and got her chocolate-covered marshmallow bunny. Then she stuck out her tongue at me.

"Next question," Mr. Klutz said as he cracked open another egg. "What's the difference between fiction and nonfiction?"

"Nonfiction has no fiction in it," I shouted. "It's like nonfat milk."

"Nonfiction is real, and fiction is a made-up story!" shouted Andrea.

"Right!" said Mr. Klutz. He gave Andrea another chocolate-covered marshmallow bunny.

Bummer in the summer! This game was no fun at all. Mr. Klutz opened another egg.

"What is above the United States?" he asked.

"The sky!" I shouted.

"Canada!" shouted Andrea.

Mr. Klutz gave Andrea *another* choco-late-covered marshmallow bunny, even though my answer was just as good as hers.

"When did Columbus discover America?" asked Mr. Klutz.

"When he stepped off the boat!" I shouted.

"In 1492!" shouted Andrea.

Another chocolate-covered marshmallow bunny for Andrea. This was a dumb game.

"Where do we get orange juice?" asked Mr. Klutz.

"From the supermarket!" I shouted.

"From oranges!" shouted Andrea.

She got *another* chocolate-covered marshmallow bunny for *that* lucky guess. She had *five* chocolate-covered marshmallow bunnies now. Nobody else had *any*. This definitely wasn't fair.

"Okay, you should get *this* one, A.J.," said Mr. Klutz. "What do they call the man who wears a striped shirt and a whistle at a football game?"

"Bob!" I shouted.

"The referee!" shouted Andrea. She got *another* chocolate-covered marshmallow bunny!

It went on like that for a while. Mr. Klutz gave out all the chocolate-covered marshmallow bunnies he had, and most of them went to Andrea. This was the worst thing to happen since TV Turnoff Week! Not only was Andrea getting all the chocolate-covered marshmallow bunnies, but she beat me in the contest too. I was really mad.

After it was all over, Andrea came over to me.

"I don't even *like* chocolate-covered marshmallow bunnies," she said. "You can have mine, Arlo."

"Really?" I said, taking the bag. "Thanks!"

"Oooooh!" Ryan said, "Andrea gave her chocolate-covered marshmallow bunnies to A.J. They must be in *love*!"

"When are you gonna get married?" asked Michael.

I didn't like the gang teasing me. But at least I got some chocolate-covered marshmallow bunnies, so I didn't feel so bad.

"You're really smart, Arlo," Andrea whispered in my ear as I was eating a chocolate-covered marshmallow bunny. "Your problem is that you think outside the box too much."*

---

*Why is everybody always talking about boxes? And why is everybody thinking inside and outside of them?

Run for It!

It was getting late. The servants started picking up the kites, Hula-Hoops, and other things off the lawn. The face painters, jugglers, banjo players, and storytellers packed up their stuff to leave. The big lawn looked perfect for a football game again.

"Well, it has been a lovely day," Mayor Hubble announced. "Thank you for coming to Hubble Manor."

"See you all next Easter," said Mrs. Bubbles. "Tah tah!"

People started making their way toward the driveway.

"Wait a minute," said one of the parents. "We didn't find the golden egg yet."

"Yeah, nobody found the golden egg," said another parent.

"You said there are ten hundred-dollar bills inside it," said a third parent.

"Did I say that?" asked Mayor Hubble. "Ha-ha. Well, I was just joking."

"That's right," Mrs. Bubbles said. "The mayor was just joking around. He's always saying silly things like that. He's such a comedian!"

"It didn't sound like a joke to me," said a parent.

"I'm not leaving here until I find that egg," one of the other parents said.

That's when I saw the most amazing thing in the history of the world. Mayor Hubble took something out of his pocket like he didn't want anyone to notice. He was slipping it into Mrs. Bubbles's hand. But neither of them was looking down, and they dropped the thing on the grass.

It was the golden egg!

Mayor Hubble was going to keep the thousand dollars for *himself*! What a scam!

"There it is!" I shouted. "The golden egg!"

"The Hubbles have been hiding it the

whole time!" shouted Alexia.

"Run for it, Bubbles!" Mayor Hubble yelled. Then he picked the golden egg up off the grass and started running.

"Get them!" somebody shouted.

Mayor Hubble and Bubbles Hubble were running across the lawn to where the helicopter was sitting. The mayor ran fast for an old guy. And Mrs. Bubbles moved pretty well for a lady wearing high heels.

The Hubbles were at the twenty-yard line! The thirty-yard line! Kids and parents were running after them. Some of the kids were throwing eggs, malted milk balls, and jelly beans at them.

The Hubbles were at the forty-yard line! They were at midfield!

The propellers of the helicopter started spinning around.

"They stole the golden egg!" somebody shouted. "They're escaping!"

"Stop those criminals!" shouted somebody else.

Everybody was chasing Mayor Hubble and Mrs. Bubbles. They were at the

thirty-yard line! The twenty-five-yard line! It looked like they were going to make it to the helicopter and get away!

But you'll never believe in a million hundred years who came charging out of nowhere.

It was the Easter Bunny!

Boomer Wiggins—in his Easter Bunny

costume—was dashing across the field at full speed! I never saw a man run so fast! Or a bunny. You should have *been* there!

Just before Mayor Hubble reached the helicopter, Boomer took a flying leap and tackled him. A bunch of other people tackled Mrs. Bubbles.

"Oooof!" Mayor Hubble grunted as he hit the ground. The golden egg slipped out of his hand.

"Fumble!" we all shouted.

A bunch of us kids pounced on the golden egg. It cracked open, and the hundred-dollar bills went flying everywhere. The grown-ups were crawling all over on their hands and knees to get them.

"Somebody call the police," yelled Boomer Wiggins, who was sitting on top of Mayor Hubble.

"I'm innocent, I tell you!" Mayor Hubble shouted.

"I was going to *give* you the golden egg!" said Bubbles. "I really *was*."

"Tell it to the cops," said Boomer. "Hey boys, we need something to tie up these two creeps. Can I use your ties?"

"Sure!" we all said, ripping those dumb ties off our necks.

Boomer used our ties to tie Mayor Hubble's and Bubbles Hubble's arms behind their backs.

A few minutes later, a police car arrived with the siren blasting. Boomer told the police what happened.

"Good work, Boomer," one of the policemen said. "Have you ever thought about joining the police force?"

"Come with me, Mayor," said the other policeman. "You and your wife are going to jail for a *long* time."

"But . . . but . . . but . . ."

We all giggled because "but" sounds just like "butt" even though it only has one "t." Grown-ups always get mad when you say "butt." Nobody knows why.

The policemen shoved Mayor Hubble and Bubbles Hubble into the back of the police car. Nah-nah-nah boo-boo on them.

"Hooray for Boomer Wiggins!" I shouted. "He's the best Easter Bunny *ever*!"

"He's our hero!" shouted Alexia.

"Can I have your autograph?" asked Neil.

"Hip-hip hooray!" said Ryan. "Hip-hip hooray!"

After it was all over, we had a fancy dinner with ham, mac-and-cheese, poached eggs, and hot cross buns. Yum! It was almost as good as candy.

Maybe Mayor Hubble will stay in jail this time. Maybe I'll start wearing a tie in case anybody needs to be tied up. Maybe Boomer Wiggins will stop eating junk food and become a policeman. Maybe next Easter we'll get some Peeps and some *real* Chinese food instead of an egg roll. Maybe grown-ups will stop drinking coffee, standing behind podiums, and talking about the weather all the time. Maybe Mr.

Klutz will be able to get the dye off his head. Maybe people will stop walking into doors and climbing in and out of boxes all the time. Maybe Mayor Hubble will go to a doctor and try to solve his bathroom problem. Maybe they'll start making tuxedos for penguins. Maybe Little Bunny Foo Foo will stop hurting poor, defenseless field mice who were minding their own business. Maybe I'll talk Ryan into eating a sugar-coated dirt clump.

But it won't be easy!

MY
WeiRd
SchooL
SPECIAL

Bunny Double, We're in Trouble!

WEIRD EXTRAS!

★ Professor A.J.'s Weird Easter Facts

★ Fun Games and Weird-Word Puzzles

★ My Weird School Trivia Questions

★ The World of Dan Gutman Checklist

PROFESSOR A.J.'S WEIRD EASTER FACTS

Howdy, My Weird School fanatics! This is your old pal Professor A.J. Since I'm in the gifted and talented program at school, I know a lot of stuff that normal kids like you don't know. So nah-nah-nah boo-boo on you!

Today I'm going to tell you a bunch of stuff you probably don't know about Easter. Like this, for instance . . .

Back in ancient times, when springtime came, cavemen would scatter colored eggs around so animals would come and eat them. Then, while the animals were eating the eggs, the cavemen would leap out with spears and kill the animals for food. That's how the tradition of the Easter egg hunt and Easter dinner got started.

Okay, I totally made that up. Cavemen Easter egg hunts? Man, you'll fall for *anything*! I bet that if I told you the Easter Bunny came from Mars, you would believe it.*

But here's some real, *true* stuff about Easter that I found out by spending a million hundred hours doing research (okay, okay, I typed "Google"). . . .

---

*Don't believe everything you read just because it's written in a book. Especially if it's written in a My Weird School book!

If you ask me, Easter should make up its mind, like Christmas. Christmas is always on the same day: December 25. Easter doesn't even know what *month* it's in. What a dumbhead! Can you imagine if your birthday was a different day every year? That would be weird.

(And that's just in *my* house.) We eat more candy on Easter than we do on Christmas. We eat more candy on Easter than we do on Valentine's Day! The only day we eat *more* candy is on Halloween (the best day of the year).

That's a lot of Peeps! I think I ate 700 million Peeps last Easter. I thought I was gonna die. It was the greatest day of my life.

If you think 700 million Peeps is impressive, every Easter we eat 16 *billion* jelly beans! Wow! If you took all those jelly beans and put them in a line next to each other, do you know how far they would reach? Me neither. But that would be a really weird thing to do. Anybody who lines up jelly beans has too much time on his hands.

FACT:

—The first time in the history of the world that the Easter Bunny was mentioned was back in the seventeenth century, in Germany. So the Easter Bunny is over four hundred years old.

Wow! That's almost as old as my parents.

FACT:

—The first White House Easter Egg Roll was back in 1878, when Rutherford B. Hayes was president. He was also the first president to use a telephone.

Do you know what President Hayes said during his first phone call? He said, "Is this the police? Come to the White House right away. There are a bunch of people rolling eggs all over my lawn! Get them out of here!"

FACT:

—According to the *Guinness Book of World Records*, the largest Easter egg in the history of the world was over twenty-five feet high and weighed almost nine thousand pounds.

If you think that's big, just imagine the size of the chicken.

"Easter" rhymes with "keister." Do you know what a keister is? A keister is your butt. You can't say "butt," because grown-ups get mad. Nobody knows why. But it's perfectly okay to say "keister." So the next time you want to say "butt," say "keister" instead. If your parents get mad, just tell them they should be glad you didn't say "butt."

I could tell you a lot more cool stuff about Easter, but I have more important things to do. Like go stuff my face with Peeps and chocolate bunnies and jelly beans. Happy Easter!

Professor A.J. (the professor of awesomeness)

FUN GAMES AND WEIRD-WORD PUZZLES

HOPPY EASTER MAZE

Directions: The golden egg has been hidden somewhere in Mayor Hubble's backyard. Help A.J. find it first! But don't get distracted by the ordinary eggs hidden along the way.

EASTER WORD HUNT

Directions: There are ten Easter words hiding in this messy jumble of letters. Can you find them all?

```
Z C X H K C A N D Y L N T D E
V H D J H N D D B X W I P F G
W O F G A E Q C L G U C I S S
L C G U D F L O W E R S H L M
J O G Q L S K J D V X P E K Y
G L E A O M F V E N C R W N E
V A K C P B S E M C H I C K W
D T B N D A E X K R N N A V S
E E G G W S U U F Y C G X S O
Q E G D G K V D S U D J C W C
D D S P S E M J E P S D B O T
B O N N E T D H U N T R F R R
X U D I C E W K I Q M W K E W
C E H R E U U E R E H R E P S
J D V E Y P I B U N N Y D W A
```

**BUNNY BASKET EGG CHOCOLATE CANDY
CHICK SPRING FLOWERS HUNT BONNET**

HIDDEN EASTER EGGS

Directions: There are two decorated Easter eggs hidden on this page! Connect the dots in number order until you reveal the invisible images, then color in the eggs any way you'd like.

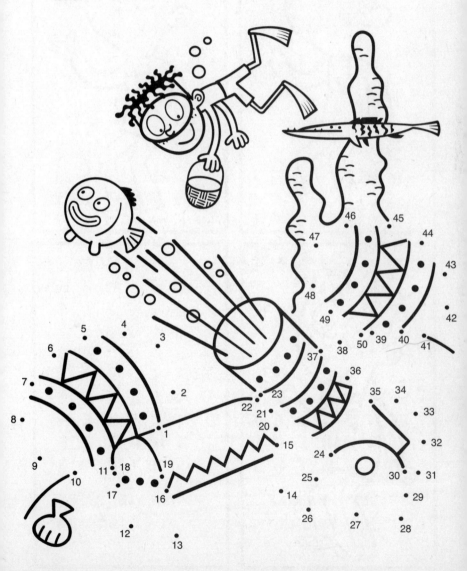

DRAW YOUR OWN MY WEIRD SCHOOL CHARACTER!

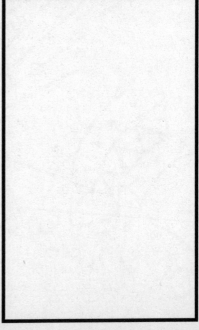

EGGSTRAORDINARY EASTER CODE

Directions: Use this secret code to swap in letters below and help A.J. solve these Easter mysteries!

A	B	C	D	E	F	G	H	I	J
H	D	L	Q	C	K	W	E	J	P

K	L	M	N	O	P	Q	R	S	T
G	O	Y	B	N	T	R	F	X	Z

U	V	W	X	Y	Z
I	S	M	V	U	A

Who's hiding inside the bunny suit?

___ ___ ___ ___ ___ ___

___ ___ ___ ___ ___ ___ ___

D	N	N	Y	C	F
M	J	W	W	J	B	X

Who stole the golden egg?

___ ___ ___ ___ ___

___ ___ ___ ___ ___ ___

Y	H	U	N	F
E	I	D	D	O	C

EASTER EGG SCRAMBLE

Directions: Words can do weird things when you scramble them! See how many smaller words you can make from the letters in these bigger words. Try to come up with at least ten smaller words for each!

Here's an example:

MY WEIRD SCHOOL

1. DREW
2. MOWS
3. SOME

CHOCOLATE CANDY	EASTER BUNNY	GOLDEN EGG
1	1	1
2	2	2
3	3	3
4	4	4
5	5	5
6	6	6
7	7	7
8	8	8
9	9	9
10	10	10

MY WEIRD SCHOOL
TRIVIA QUESTIONS

There's no way in a million hundred years you'll get all these answers right. So nah-nah-nah boo-boo on you!

Q: WHY DID GROWN-UPS THINK UP THE IDEA OF SCHOOL, ACCORDING TO A.J.?

A: So they wouldn't have to pay babysitters anymore

Q: WHAT DOES ANDREA'S MOTHER DO FOR A LIVING?

A: She's a psychologist.

Q: WHAT FLOOR OF ELLA MENTRY SCHOOL IS THE DUNGEON ON?

A: Third

Q: WHICH STAFF MEMBER INVENTED A SECRET LANGUAGE THAT MAKES NO SENSE?

A: Mrs. Kormel

Q: WHO DOES ANDREA'S MOTHER PLAY TENNIS WITH?

A: A.J.'s mother

Q: WHAT'S IN THE MIDDLE OF THE LIBRARY?

A: A giant tree

Q: WHAT DO GROWN-UPS ALWAYS DO WHEN THEY'RE MAD?

A: Put their hands on their hips

Q: WHAT DO GROWN-UPS ALWAYS DO WHEN THEY'RE THINKING?

A: They rub their forehead.

Q: HOW OLD IS MR. LORING?

A: A million hundred years old

Q: WHAT DOES ANDREA'S MOTHER LOOK LIKE?

A: Andrea, with wrinkles

Q: WHAT WAS IN THE GOODY BAG AT ANDREA'S BIRTHDAY PARTY?

A: Tea bags

Q: WHAT DOES MR. DOCKER USE TO HAMMER IN A NAIL?

A: A banana

Q: WHY SHOULD YOU EAT DESSERT BEFORE YOUR MEAL?

A: If an asteroid hits the earth in the middle of lunch and destroys the planet, at least you got to eat dessert.

Q: WHAT DID A.J.'S FRIEND BILLY DRESS UP AS ON HALLOWEEN?

A: The Underwearwolf

Q: WHAT DID A.J. GIVE EMILY AS A SECRET SANTA PRESENT?

A: A bag of dead fish

Q: WHO WAS MR. MACKY'S FAVORITE PRESIDENT?

A: Millard Fillmore

Q: WHO DOES A.J. DO HIS PRESIDENTS' DAY ORAL REPORT ON?

A: Benjamin Franklin

Q: WHY DON'T THEY INVITE DR. SEUSS TO VISIT ELLA MENTRY SCHOOL?

A: Because he's dead

Q: WHAT DOES MRS. YONKERS WEAR ON HER HEAD?

A: A large piece of cheese

Q: HOW DOES MRS. YONKERS TYPE ON A COMPUTER?

A: With her feet

Q: WHAT DOES A.J. USE TO STEAL DR. CARBLES'S TOUPEE?

A: A fishing pole

Q: WHAT WAS DR. CARBLES'S NICKNAME WHEN HE WAS A TEENAGER?

A: Walrus Face

Q: WHAT DOES MR. LOUIE USE FOR A STOP SIGN?

A: The back of his guitar

ANSWER KEY

HOPPY EASTER MAZE

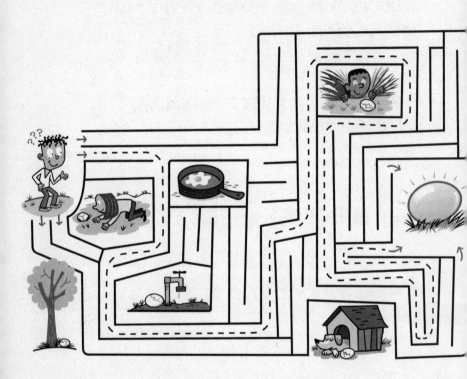

EASTER WORD HUNT

```
Z C X H K C A N D Y L N T D E
V H D J H N D D B X W I P F G
W O F G A E Q C L G U C I S S
L C G U D F L O W E R S H L M
J G G Q L S K J D V X P E K Y
G E A O M F V E N C R W N E
V L K C P B S E M C H I C K
D A B N D A E X K R N A V S
E T E G G W S U U F Y C G X S O
Q E G D G K V D S U D J C W C
D D S P S E M J E P S D B O T
B O N N E T D H U N T R F R R
X U D I C E W K I Q M W K E W
C E H R E U U E R E H R E P S
J D V E Y P I B U N N Y D W A
```

HIDDEN EASTER EGGS

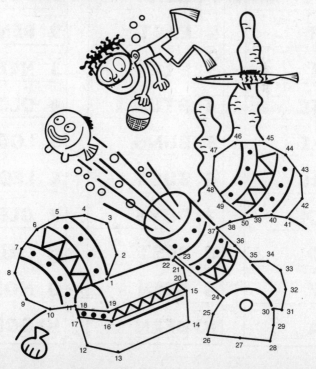

EGGSTRAORDINARY
EASTER CODE

Who's hiding inside the bunny suit?

B O O M E R   W I G G I N S

Who stole the golden egg?

M A Y O R   H U B B L E

EASTER EGG SCRAMBLE

CHOCOLATE CANDY	EASTER BUNNY	GOLDEN EGG
1 LATE	1 SUN	1 DOG
2 HOT	2 EAST	2 DEN
3 DOT	3 STAR	3 NEED
4 DATE	4 STUB	4 OLD
5 TALE	5 BUNS	5 LOG
6 DEAL	6 BUST	6 LEG
7 COOL	7 BUYS	7 GLEN
8 HAD	8 BEST	8 GEL
9 DAY	9 BEEN	9 NODE
10 TEA	10 BEAN	10 GONE

THE WORLD OF DAN GUTMAN CHECKLIST

MY WEIRD SCHOOL

MY WEIRD SCHOOL DAZE

MY WEIRDER SCHOOL

MY WEIRD SCHOOL SPECIAL

THE GENIUS FILES